Book Publishers Network
P. O. Box 2256
Bothell, WA 98041
425-483-3040
www.bookpublishersnetwork.com

10 9 8 7 6 5 4 3 2 1

Printed in the United States of America

LCCN: 2016932554
ISBN: 978-1-940598-94-9

Special Dedication

To the Phillips family, your generosity has made a life changing experience for us and potentially many more. It is our honor to call you our friends and to have your support. Thank you for believing in our dream. We will do everything in our power to make sure that *The Adventures of Frank and Mustard* succeeds.

Executive Producers

The Phillips Family, Eric Chase

Producer Credits

New Hope Ministry Center, Erin Gillet, Tom & Lynette Batson, Vicki Hall, The Magnusson Family, Courtney Drennon, Jillian Davidson, Lynn, Julie Godden

Special Thanks

9

13

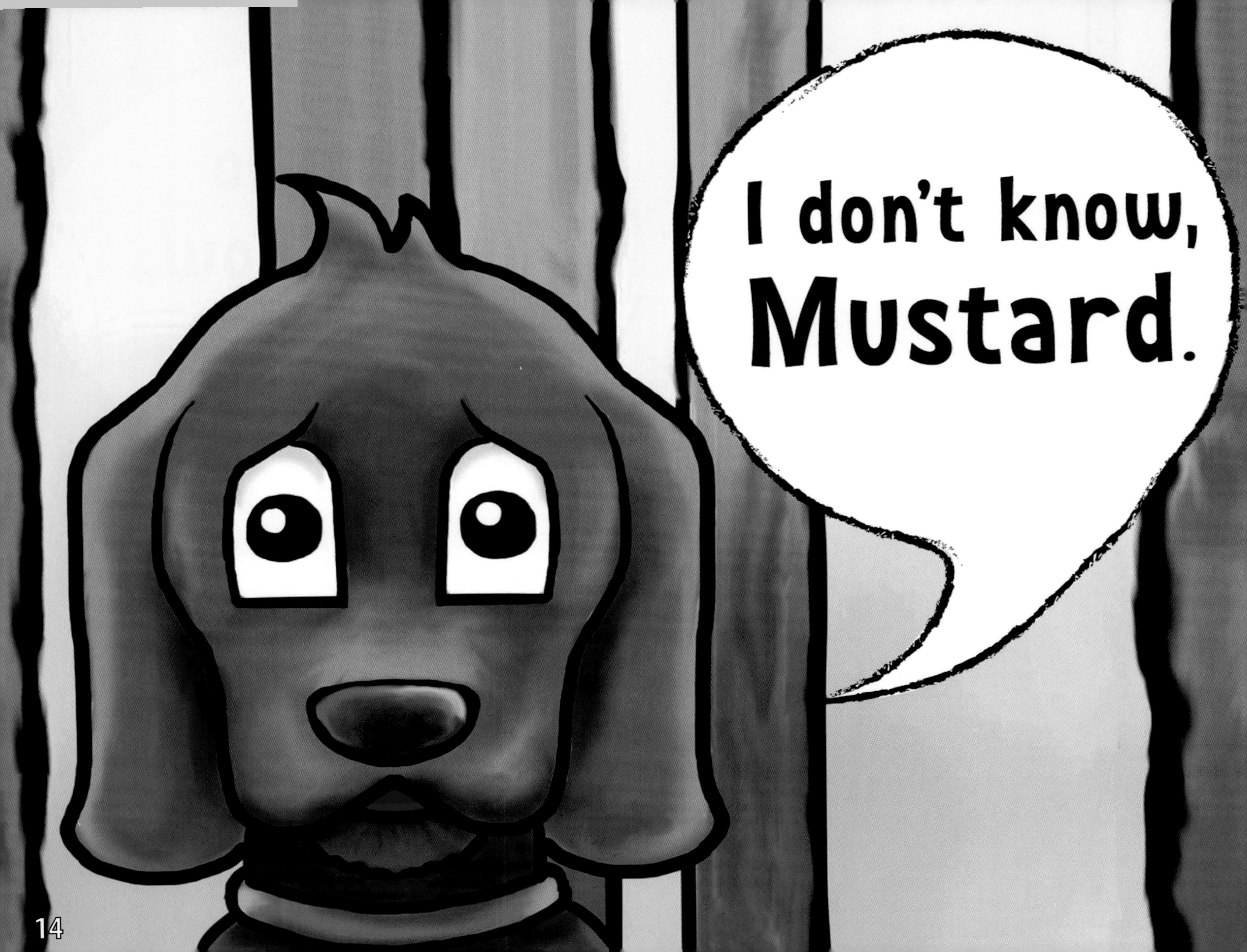
I don't know, Mustard.

15

17

19

What are we going to do now, Mustard?

21

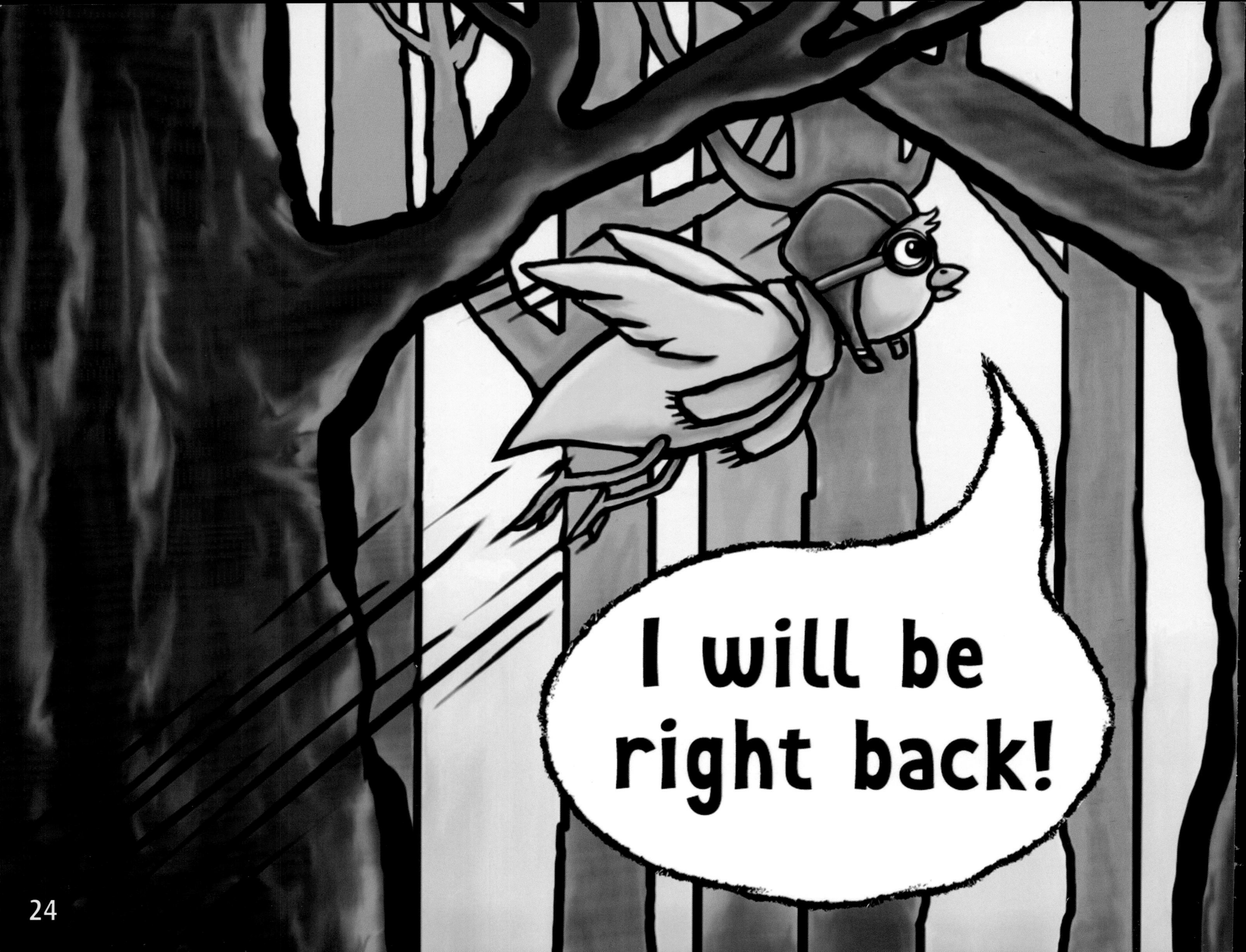
I will be right back!

25

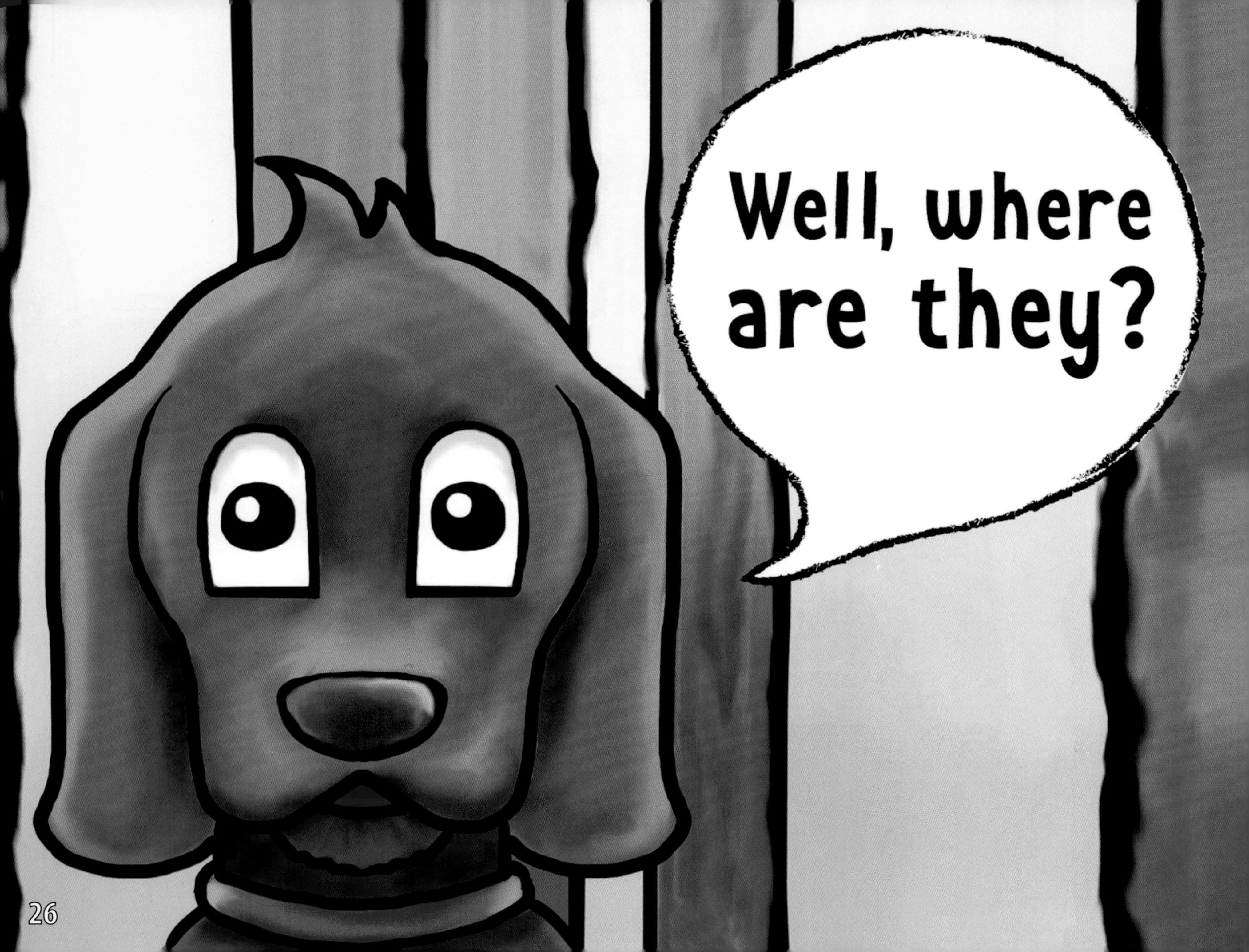
Well, where are they?

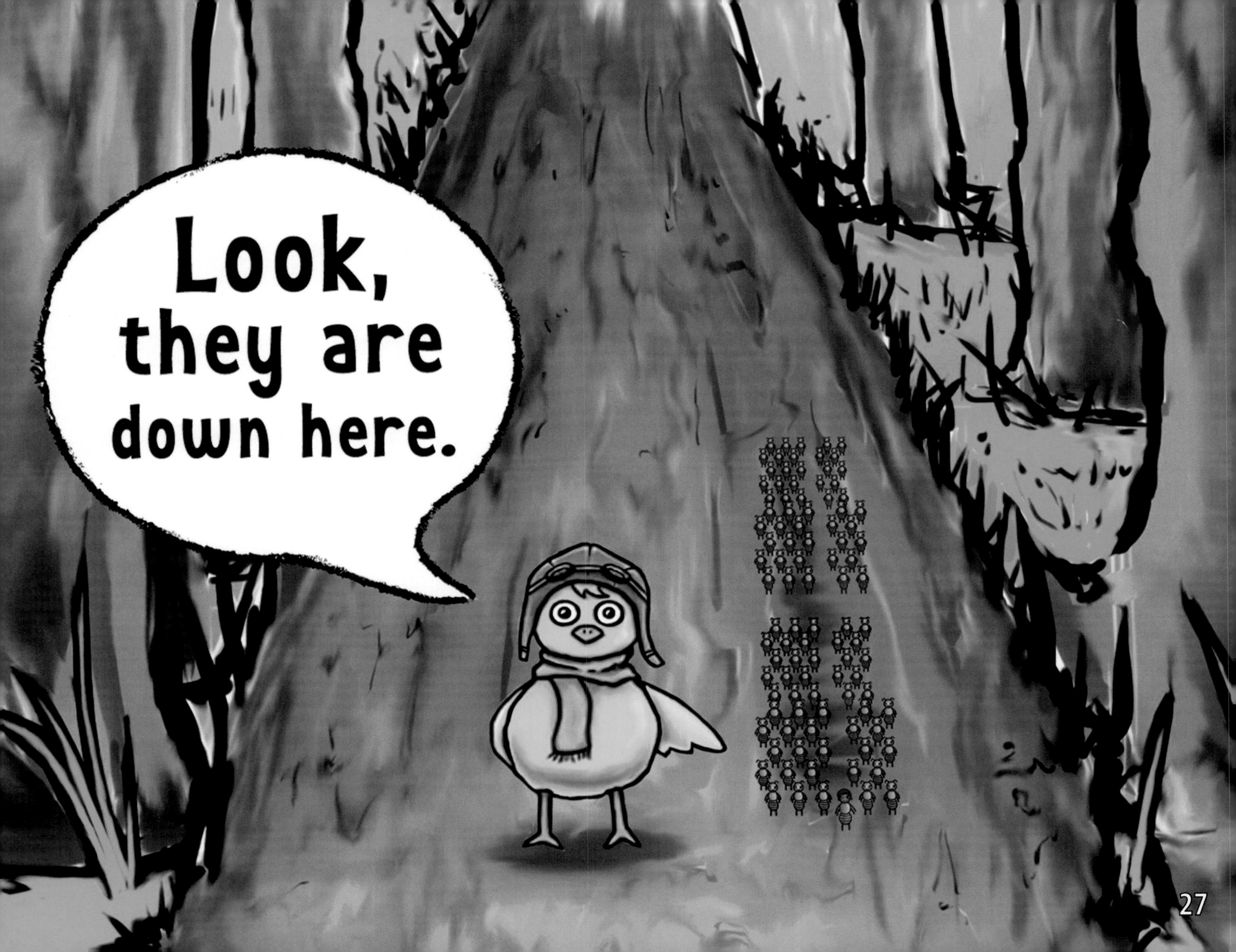
Look, they are down here.

Sergeant Ant, at your service!

29

33

Hold on Frank, I'll come back with more help.

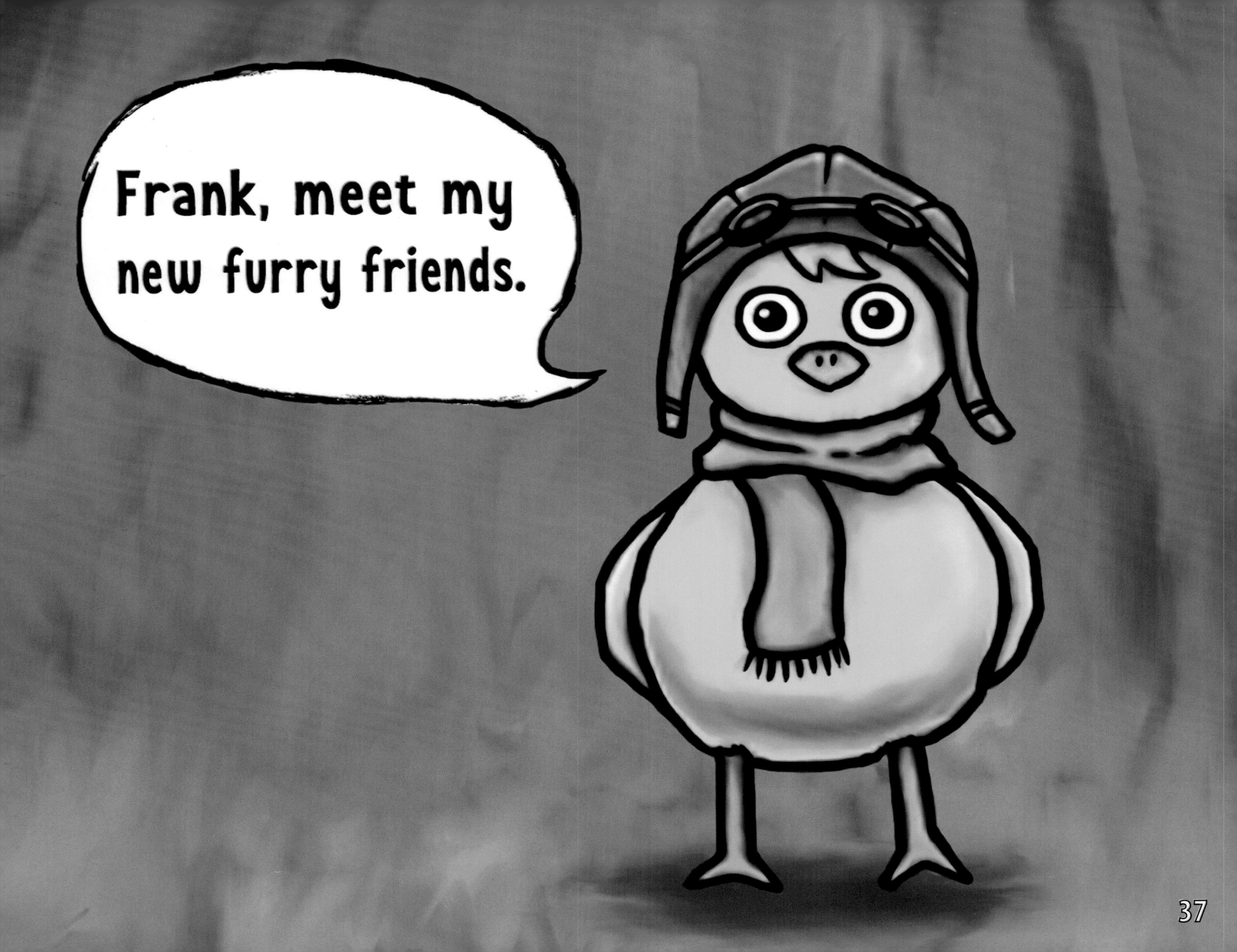
Frank, meet my new furry friends.

39

Heave-ho! Heave-ho! Heave-ho!

43

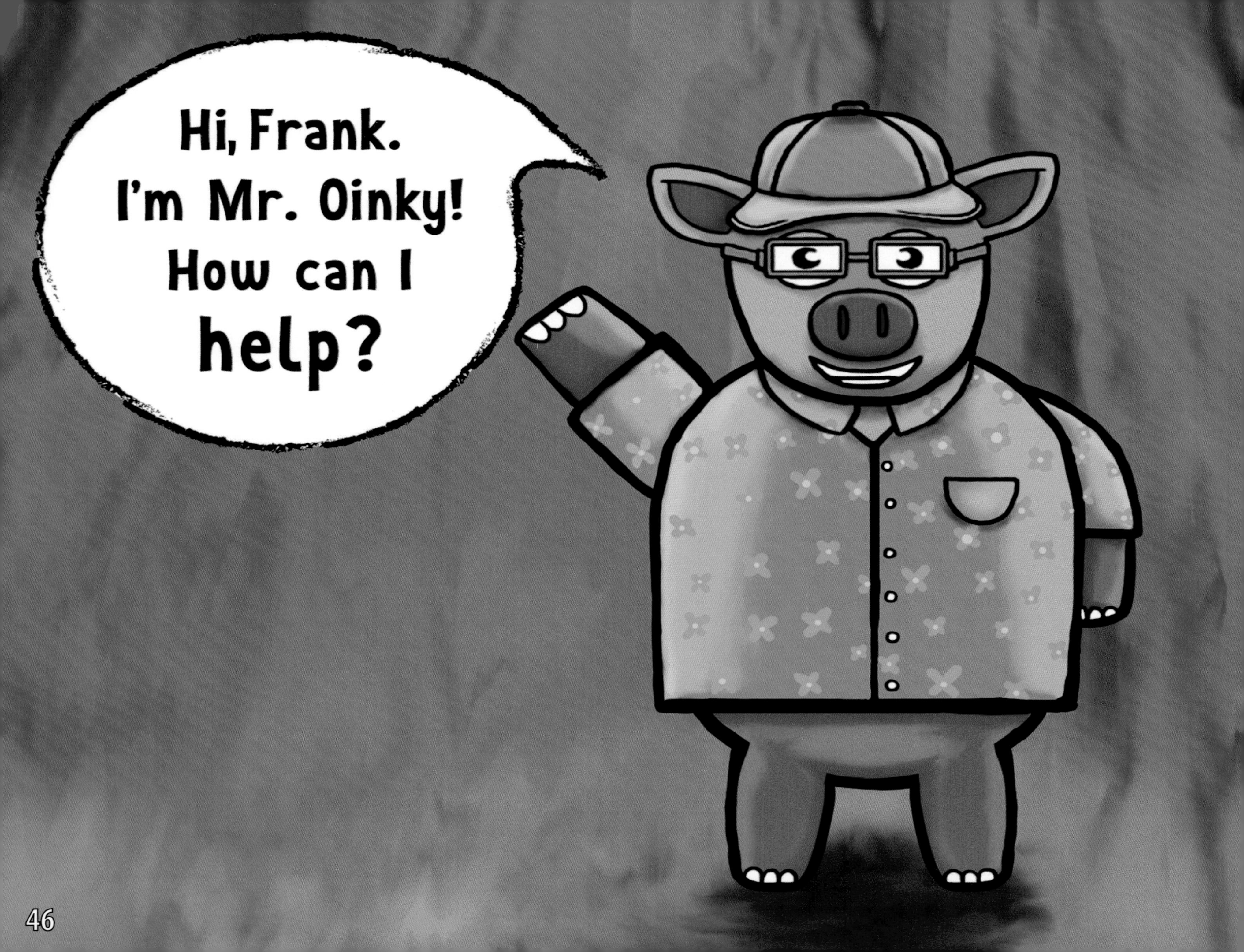
Hi, Frank.
I'm Mr. Oinky!
How can I
help?

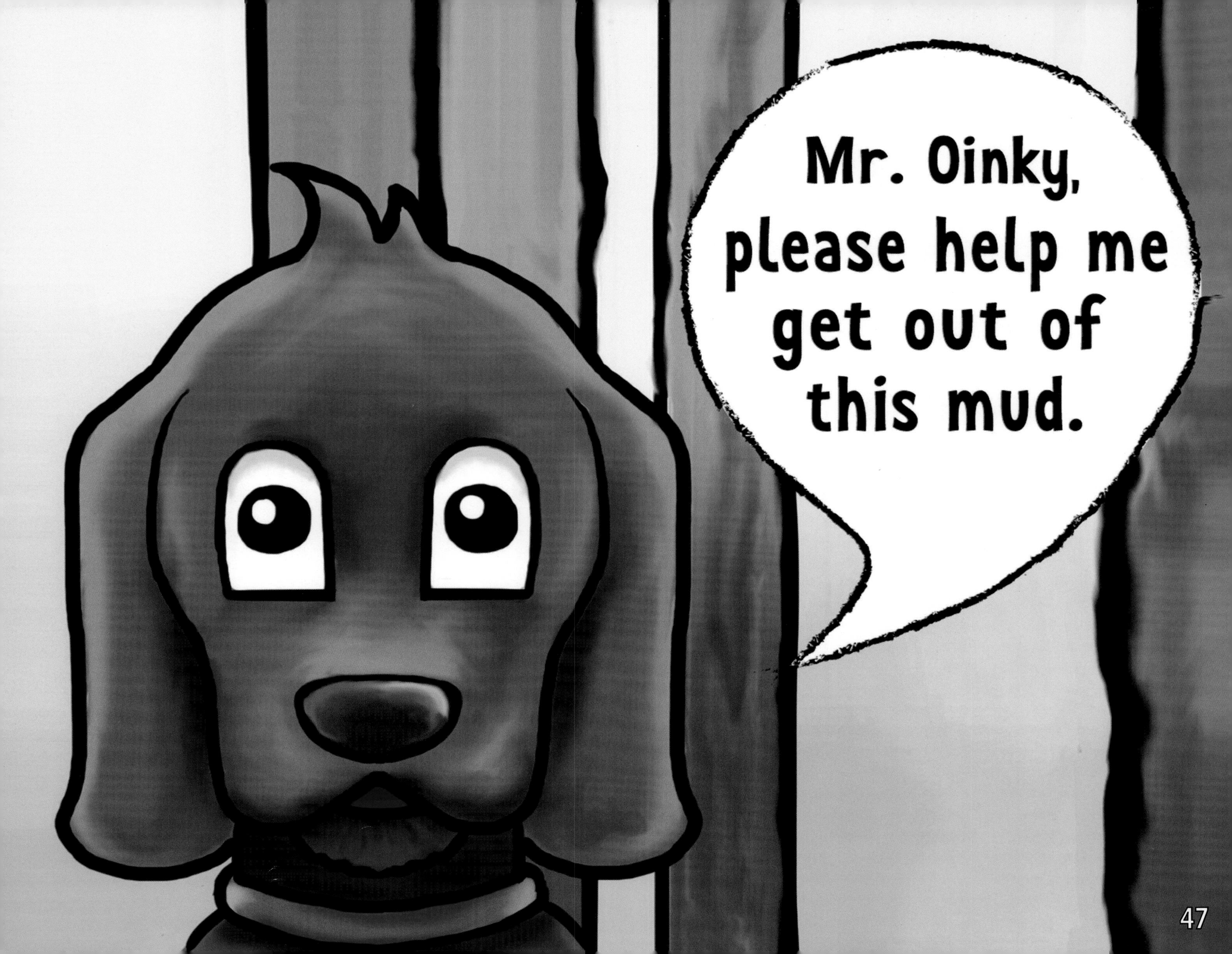
Mr. Oinky, please help me get out of this mud.

49

1. What did you enjoy most about reading this book?

2. Who is your favorite character? Why?

3. What are some of the things that you learned from this book?

4. How do you think Frank felt after getting stuck in the mud?

5. Have you ever experienced anything similar to being stuck in the mud?

6. What would you do if you were stuck in a similar situation and needed help?

7. What would you do if you saw someone who was stuck and needed help?

8. What is your favorite ice cream?